SNAKES
ON THE
JOB

KATHRYN DENNIS

WALKER BOOKS
AND SUBSIDIARIES
LONDON · BOSTON · SYDNEY · AUCKLAND

For little builders everywhere

First published in Great Britain in 2022 by Walker Books Ltd
87 Vauxhall Walk, London SE11 5HJ

First published in Canada and the USA in 2020 by Feiwel and Friends,
an imprint of Macmillan Publishing Group, LLC
175 Fifth Avenue, New York, United States, 10010

2 4 6 8 10 9 7 5 3 1

© 2020 Kathryn Dennis

The right of Kathryn Dennis to be identified as author of this work has been asserted
in accordance with the Copyright, Designs and Patents Act 1988

This book has been typeset in Loose Thin

Printed in China

British Library Cataloguing in Publication Data:
a catalogue record for this book is available from the British Library

ISBN 978-1-5295-0760-7

www.walker.co.uk

Off to work the snakes will go.

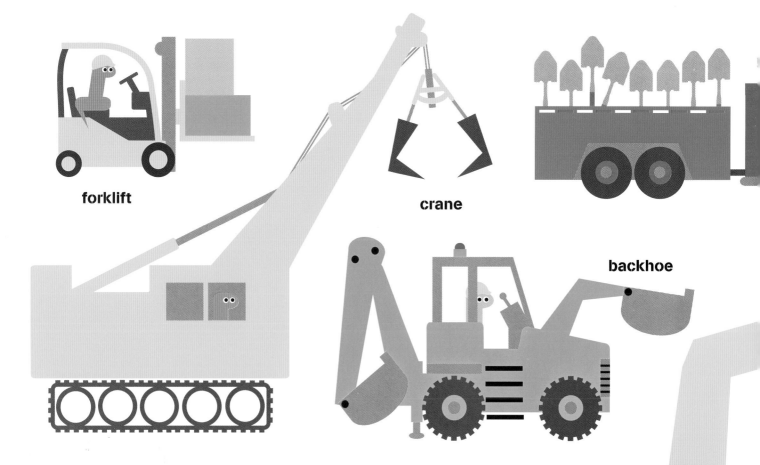

forklift

crane

backhoe

They slide into trucks
and roll out slow.

digger/excavator

PLAYTIME

delivery van

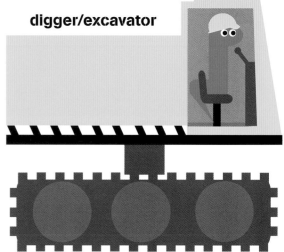

pick-up truck and trailer

bulldozer

food truck

dump truck

loader

Hisssssssssssssh goes the sound of the brakes.

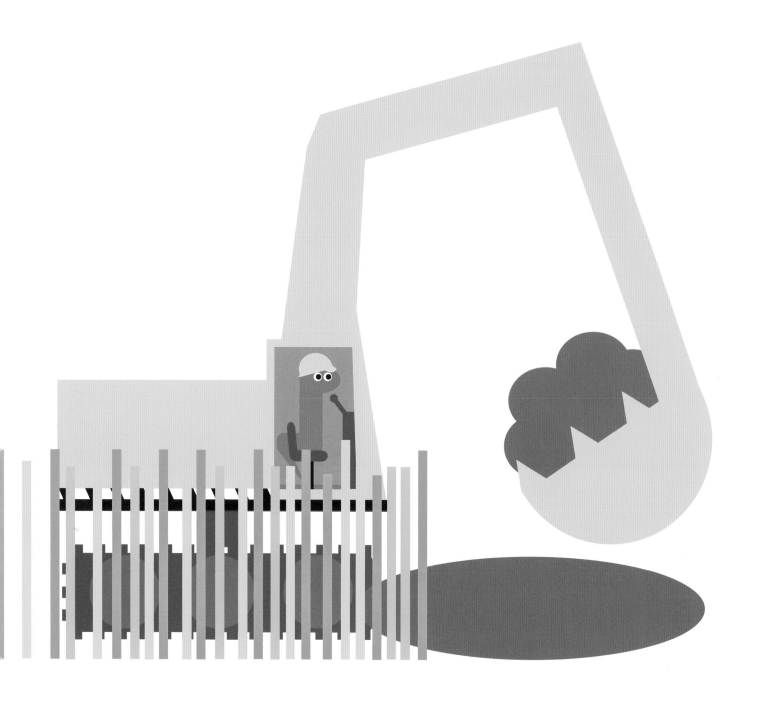

A digger clears the way

as a bulldozer shoves the dirt to one side.

Dump trucks are piled high.

Hisssssssssssssh goes the sound of the brakes.

A row of delivery vans

keeps snakes moving at a steady pace.

A crane lifts large objects and swings them into place.

Hissssssssssh goes the sound of the brakes.

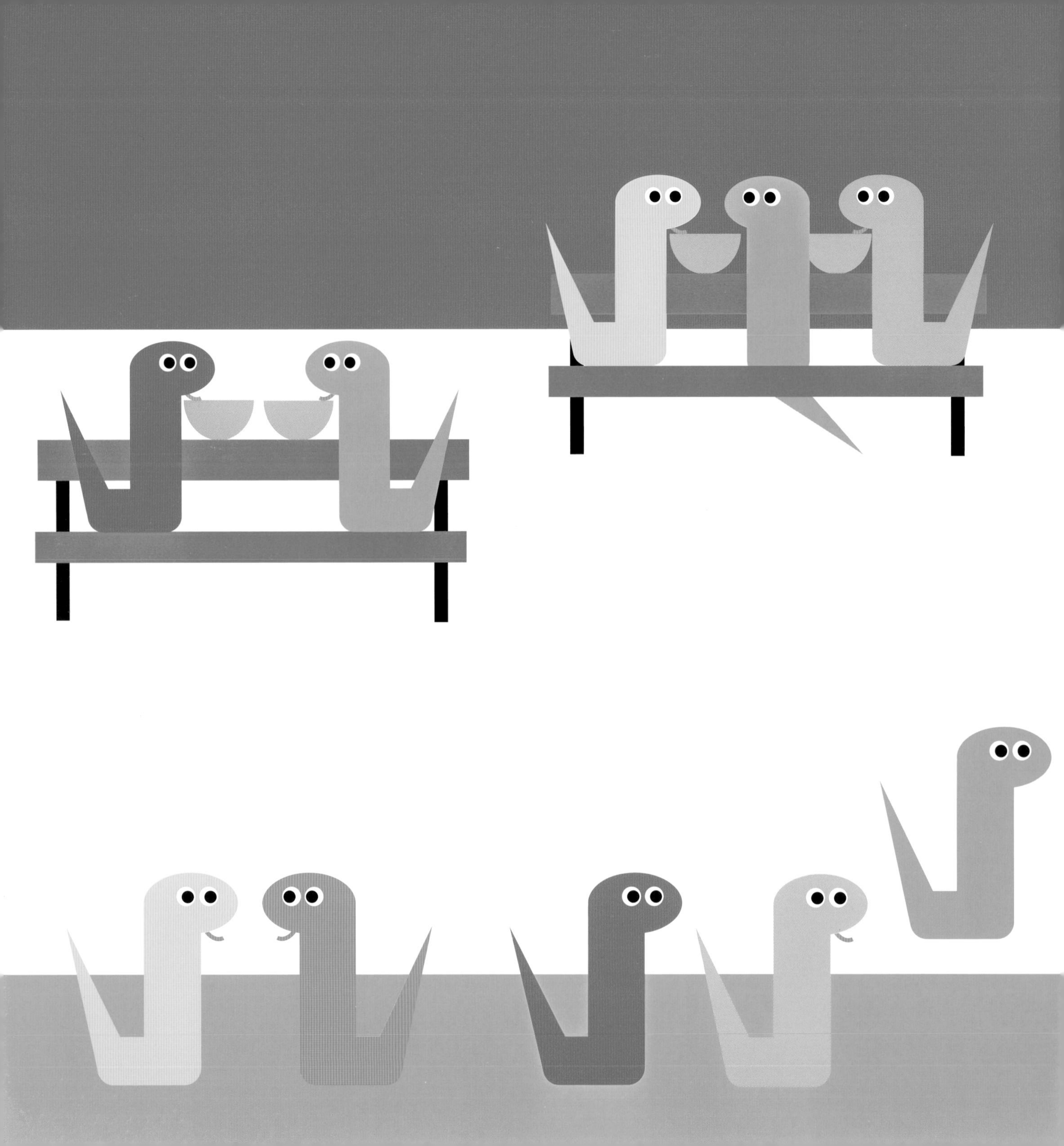

A food truck arrives and the
snakes line up for lunch.

Then it's back to work.

There's a time crunch.

Now a loader rumbles in. Holes are dug
and flowers fill wheelbarrows.

Hisssssssssssssh goes the sound of the brakes.

It takes three snakes to roll

a giant wheel into place.

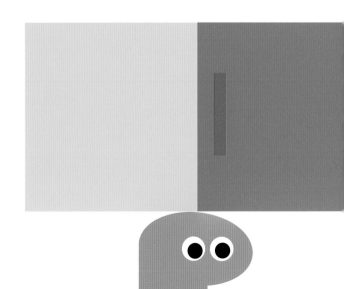

Snakes work together to reach their goal.

A backhoe is needed to put in posts.
The project is coming to a close.

Hissssssssssssssh goes the sound of the brakes.

It's time to see what the snakes have built.

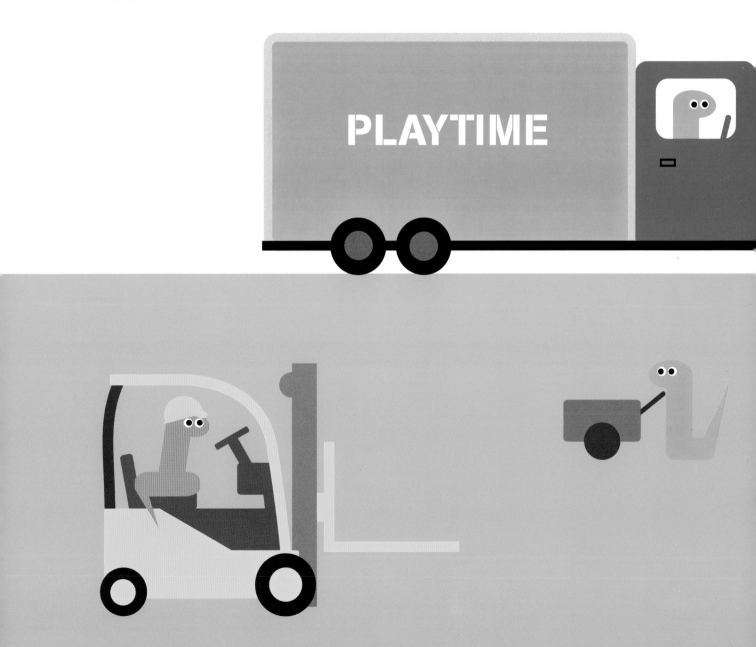

Hisssssssssssh **go the happy snakes.**

Hamsters ask if they can play.
What will the snakes say?

WELCOME!

Yesssssssssssh.